Cock-A-Doodle Christmas!

Written and Illustrated by

Will Hillenbrand

Marshall Cavendish Children

To Noah

Text and illustrations copyright © 2007 by Will Hillenbrand

Marshall Cavendish, 99 White Plains Road, Tarrytown, NY 10591
www.marshallcavendish.us/kids

Library of Congress Cataloging-in-Publication Data
Hillenbrand, Will.
Cock-a-doodle Christmas! / by Will Hillenbrand. — 1st ed.
p. cm.
Summary: Long ago in the town of Bethlehem, young Harold the rooster
keeps failing to wake the other farm animals in the morning,
but when a young woman gives birth to a very special baby in the stable,
Harold is finally able to crow loudly and help spread the good news.
ISBN 978-0-7614-5354-3
[1. Roosters—Fiction. 2. Domestic animals—Fiction.
3. Jesus Christ—Nativity—Fiction. 4. Christmas—Fiction.] I. Title.
PZ7.H55773Coc 2007
[E]—dc22
2006030236

The text of this book is set in Mrs Eaves.
The illustrations are rendered in designers gouache, ink and collage on gessoed canvas.
Book design by Vera Soki
Editor: Margery Cuyler

Printed in Malaysia
First edition
1 3 5 6 4 2
Marshall Cavendish
Children

Long ago, in the village of Bethlehem, a group of animals lived happily together on a farm.

Every morning, Old Rooster crowed.

Cock-A-Doodle-Doo!

When the farm animals heard his cock-a-doodle-doo, they knew it was time to start their day.

Hen would lay an egg. Cow would give milk.

Donkey would tote his cart.

Ox would pull the plow.

But Old Rooster was getting tired. Soon he would be retiring and moving to another farm to live with his sister.

"Who will take your place?" asked the animals.

"I will teach young Harold to crow," said Old Rooster.

The following day, Old Rooster gave Harold a simple lesson.

ONE. Mount the post just before dawn.

TWO. Take ten deep breaths.

THREE. Release air while crowing

COCK-A-DOODLE-DOO!

FOUR. Repeat these steps, until everyone has awakened.

"I can't do that. My voice is too small," whined Harold.

"Don't worry, Harold, you'll be GREAT,"
said Old Rooster. "I'm off to my sister's farm.
Good luck!"

Harold felt alone and unsure of himself.
He returned to the comfort of his nest,
but that didn't make him feel any better.

He knew that the next morning
he would have to wake everyone up.

When the time came, he stood on the
post, took deep breaths, and croaked:

COCK-A-DOODLE DOO!

His "cock-a-doodle-doo" was very soft. He tried again and again, but no one heard him, and no one woke up. This caused trouble for all the animals.

BAAAAK!

"I didn't lay an egg this morning," complained Hen.

MOoooo!

"I didn't give milk," moaned Cow.

HEE-HAW! HEE-HAW!

"I didn't pull my cart," grumbled Donkey.

MAAAA!

"I didn't pull the plow," bellowed Ox.

Harold worried. "What am I going to do? No matter how hard I try, I can't crow loud enough to wake everyone up."

This went on day after day until late one
evening, a young woman, great with child,
and her husband came to rest in the stable.

A bright light lit the night sky.
Harold dashed out of the stable to get
a better look. There was a dazzling
new star beaming in the heavens. In
the distance he heard the echo of
voices rejoicing in song.

Soon, startled shepherds
came from the fields to
worship the babe.

Harold wondered,
"What is going on?"

One shepherd said, "I have seen the scriptures fulfilled. GOOD NEWS! We have hope for a new day. The Prince of Peace has come."

"What does that old shepherd mean, 'hope for a new day'?" thought Harold. Day would soon dawn, and he would have to try once again to wake everyone up.

Harold turned toward the baby and discovered that the baby was looking directly at him. The infant's eyes were filled with love and understanding.

"Oh!" breathed Harold. His body tingled with joy! Never had he felt so special, so happy, and so calm. His worries faded away. Now he understood. This day and every day were going to be different.

Boldly, Harold opened his throat.
"Cock-a-doodle-doo!" he crowed.
Then . . .

Finally, he was crowing as loudly as Old
Rooster. All the animals woke up. So did
Old Rooster and his sister on the farm
down the road. "Good for Harold!" they cried.

Harold's call echoed throughout the
mountains. It sounded in the valleys.

And to this day, wherever you may be or
wherever you may go, roosters everywhere call out
the new day for all to hear and for all to know.